The Bones in the Cliff

JAMES STEVENSON

The Bones in the Cliff

GREENWILLOW BOOKS, New York

Library of Congress Cataloging-in-Publication Data

Stevenson, James (date)
    The bones in the cliff / by James Stevenson.
        p.   cm.
    Summary: Pete, a lonely and timid eleven-year-old who
has just made friends with an adventurous girl named Rootie,
hides out on Cutlass Island with his alcoholic father,
waiting for the gunman his father fears will kill him.
    ISBN 0-688-13745-8
    [1. Islands—Fiction.   2. Criminals—Fiction.
3. Family problems—Fiction.
4. Friendship—Fiction.
5. Fathers and sons—Fiction.]
I. Title.
PZ7.S84453Bo   1995
[Fic]—dc20
94-15381   CIP   AC

For Jane,

with love

Contents

The Man on the Boat

I used to like to watch the ferryboat come in to the island.

I'd ride my bike up to the meadow by the old Bayview Hotel. From there you could see the ocean spread out, and if you timed it right, there'd be a white dot moving along. As it got nearer, you could see the cars jammed together and, on the decks above, the sightseers in their bright summer clothes.

Then I'd jump on my bike and race down through the meadow to the town, and get to the landing just as the ferry came scraping into the slip, the pilings groaning and screeching. Then the cars and the people would flood off the boat, and it was like a party—people yelling and waving and greeting one another, laughing, hugging, kissing. It made me feel good just to be there.

But that was before my father told me to watch every boat—the ten o'clock, the two o'clock, the six o'clock—to notice every single person getting off, and never to look away, even for a second.

And in my hand there was always a quarter, always, just in case, so that if I saw the man— the crazy man—I could run to the pay phone and call my father.

CHAPTER 2

Rootie

One foggy afternoon after the two o'clock boat came in, and nobody special got off, I went to one of the souvenir stores on Bay Street to hang out and look at the junk—beach towels, coffee mugs, ashtrays, hats, postcards—all saying CUTLASS ISLAND on them, sometimes with a picture of a cutlass. I sort of wished I could send one of the postcards, maybe one that said CUTLASS IS FOR CUTUPS and showed women in bikinis with a patch over one eye and a pirate hat, something dopey, to my old friend Herbie in the city. He'd be surprised. We hadn't seen each other in a couple of years, not since my father and I started moving all the time. Herbie would like a card like that. But that was one of the main things I was never supposed to do, no matter what— never send a letter or a postcard to anybody.

Sometimes I'd look at all the cards just for fun, pulling them out of the big rack that squeaked when it turned, and I'd think about who I might want to send one to and what I might want to write on it. But then I'd put them back. The fact was, I didn't have any friends anymore.

On the walls of the store were lots of maps for sale: maps showing where the hotels and restaurants and bike rental places were, island maps, maps for sailors, copies of long-ago maps when explorers didn't draw the shape of the island right. One map gave me a chill to look at. It showed where dozens of ships had been wrecked on the island. The names and the dates were crammed in all around the coast. *Corsair*, 1734, *Mollie B.*, 1937, *Nathaniel Cook*, 1814, *Global Maru*, 1965, *Dauntless*, 1788—on and on, and there was no empty space.

I wondered why anybody would want to buy that map and stick it on their wall. When you went to the beach to swim, wouldn't you sometimes think of all the hundreds, maybe thousands of people who died there? I could imagine terrible storms—snow and thunder and broken masts, and in a flash of lightning the bodies of dead people cartwheeling in on the toppling waves.

There was a popping noise behind me. I turned fast. First I saw the big blue sunglasses, then the pink bubble-gum bubble getting bigger. *Pop!* The girl took off her sunglasses and started to peel bits of gum off the lenses.

"Jumpy?" she said. She had brown eyes.

"I was looking at the map," I said. That was lame.

"I didn't mean to surprise you," she said.

"That's okay," I said.

I'd seen her before. She was kind of a tomboy, about my age—eleven, maybe twelve. Short black hair, skinny as a stick, funny grin. I'd watched her go rocketing through town on her ten-speed, cutting in and out of traffic, jumping her bike onto the sidewalk, scattering tourists, then bouncing back into the street, never slowing down. She didn't seem to care what anybody thought.

She was wearing a T-shirt with a picture of a bottle on it. I GOT WRECKED ON CUTLASS ISLAND, it said.

"You live on Wampanoag Road, don't you?" she said. "I live right down the road from you. I come every summer."

"Which house?" I said.

"The big yellow one," she said. "It's my grand-mother's. Bowditch. There's a little sign by the stone wall. You must have moved in during the winter."

"May," I said.

"I just got new tattoos," she said, holding up a plastic package. "Dragons. What do you think?"

"Excellent," I said.

"What's your name?" she said.

"Pete. What's yours?"

"You can call me Rootie."

"Rootie?" I said. "What's that? Like Ruthie?"

"No," she said. "Never mind." She looked at the maps on the wall. "Ever been to Blackbeard's Cove?"

"No," I said. "Where is it?"

"Not too far from Wampanoag Road. Across the big meadow, over the cliff. It's the coolest beach. I could show you. Want to go?"

CHAPTER 3
___

Blackbeard's Cove

Rootie was whipping along through the mist on Wampanoag Road. I had to pedal hard to keep up. My bike was a rusty old secondhand mountain bike, and hers was brand-new with lots of gears. A few hundred yards short of my house, Rootie turned off the road and into a stand of trees.

"We'll leave our bikes here," she said, "and pick them up later." We put the bikes down, and we walked through the woods to the field. The fog was thick now, and you couldn't see far. There wasn't much difference between the earth and the sky: It was all gray. But Rootie kept going. We walked along a dirt path, winding through the bushes.

About five minutes later Rootie said, "I think we're almost there. Be careful. If you don't see the edge of the cliff, it would be like falling off a ten-story building."

"Maybe we should do this on a clear day," I said. "And besides, I'm supposed to be back in town pretty soon."

"Are you chicken?" said Rootie.

"Me?" I said. "I can do anything you can do. Don't worry about that."

Oh, great. I'd only known Rootie for half an hour and already she'd discovered I was a coward.

"Where's the path?" I said. "I want to see that beach." If I sounded tough, maybe I'd feel tough.

Maybe.

"It's right here," said Rootie. A breeze had come up, and it was pushing the fog around. You could see things for a minute, and then you couldn't. Rootie was standing near the edge of the field, just before it disappeared. I could see places where the edge had broken off. Nothing was left but a jagged balcony of dirt and grass sticking out over the fog. You couldn't tell what part might fall off next.

Rootie pointed straight down. "I call this the Dive of Death."

I inched toward her and peered down. The cliff was nearly vertical. I could hear the sea booming below like cannon fire, and then the rattle of rocks like muskets as the surf pulled back to attack again.

"Ready?" said Rootie. "Go where I go, and don't slow down. Just keep going. Otherwise you'll get buried by a landslide. Got it?"

"No problem," I said.

"But don't go too fast or you'll trip. Then you'd bounce down the cliff and get smashed to a pulp on the rocks."

"Not too fast and not too slow," I said. "Is that what you're telling me?"

Rootie laughed. "You got it!" Then she yelled, "Geronimo!" and jumped over the edge.

In an instant Rootie was zigzagging full tilt down the cliff.

I took a deep breath and stepped off the grass. For a minute I was in midair between the field and the ocean, tilted outward, a parachute jumper without a parachute. Then my foot hit the path, and I was running and stumbling after Rootie, the earth sliding away under my feet, rocks clattering past me, and every second I thought I would lose my balance and go straight down the cliff like a loose stone.

Then I hit the flat sand, went head over heels,

and landed with a thud. I was gasping for air. But it was over.

Rootie was sitting on a boulder. "Want to try it again?" she said.

I sat up and looked around. There wasn't much beach, just a narrow strip battered by the waves.

"My grandmother says Blackbeard used this place to execute people. Pirates who tried to double-cross him. He'd have them thrown off the top of the cliff at high tide. The current is so strong it carried the bodies right out to sea. No fuss, no mess, no digging."

The wind was picking up and throwing sand around. It stung when it hit your face. The beach was gloomy, strung with tatters of fog, and the surf was whacking at the shore.

Some of the rocks looked like prehistoric crea-tures—giant lizards, maybe, buried in the sand. We walked along. The cliffs got lower. Looking up, I could see small white branches sticking out of the side of the cliff.

"What are those?" I asked.

"Bones," said Rootie. "Human bones."

"You're kidding," I said. But I could see she was right.

"It's where they buried the Indians who died of smallpox a long time ago. A mass grave. This used to be their island. Now there's not a single Indian left."

We stared at the wall of dirt and clay.

"I guess the islanders thought the Indians were gone forever," said Rootie. "But the sea keeps eating away at the cliff, and the bones are beginning to show." Rootie lowered her voice to a whisper. "The Indians are coming back," she said. "To seek revenge."

I could see round white shapes—skulls, I guess—gleaming in the cliff.

"Let's go," I said.

But Rootie wasn't ready. She kept staring at the bones.

"You can bury things, you can run away, you can try to hide," she said. "But it never works. . . . Never."

"Come *on*," I said.

"We have to climb over the rocks," said Rootie.

She led the way, jumping like a mountain goat over big boulders with the surf seething between them. We came around a corner, and the rocks ended. The beach turned smooth and wide. The sun began to burn through, and slowly houses began to take shape in the distance, and we saw colored beach umbrellas down the shore.

Looney Tunes

In May, a few days after we moved into the green bungalow on Wampanoag Road, my father sprained his ankle. He had been drinking his vodka, and he was teetering on a stepladder in his Hawaiian shirt and baggy shorts and shower shoes, putting outdoor lights—small flood-lights—on the corners of the house. The idea, I guess, was to make a kind of no-man's-land on all sides, so he could flip a switch by the stairs inside and a ring of light would spring up, pushing the darkness back, and if anybody came toward the house they'd have to walk through the light. Well, my father was half drunk, and trembly, and he kept dropping stuff and swearing. There were cardboard boxes and light bulbs and tools and wire scattered around, and when he dropped the screwdriver he lunged for it and fell off the ladder, and twisted his ankle when he hit the ground.

I ran over to where he was lying on the grass and tried to help him, but he swore at me, saying it was my fault for not holding the ladder, and that I was never any use, no good, just a goddamn bother.

Then, finally, he said, "At least give me a hand," and I helped him get up and limp to the porch steps.

In the days after that, he had to walk slowly

with a cane, and that's when it started to be my job to watch the ferryboats.

I asked my father who it was I would be looking for. How would I know him? What did he look like?

"Ordinary," said my father. "Nothing special. He could be standing next to you in a crowd, you wouldn't pay attention. Six feet plus. A little extra weight, and a cheap-looking rug on his head." He was quiet for a minute. Then he said, "The cigar. That's the main thing. Always got the cigar."

I was scared to ask the next question. I never knew when my father would suddenly get mad.

"Why does he want to hurt you?" I asked finally.

"A misunderstanding," he said. "A business thing. That's all. He's a Looney Tunes."

And he didn't say any more.

After that, I thought of the man with the cigar as Looney Tunes. In dreams, he came toward me smiling. When he got close, his face would turn into a cartoon, twisting and stretching, bulging and melting—and I would wake up in a cold sweat.

But one night it was the phone that woke me. It rang and rang. My father never heard the phone. He drank himself to sleep. I stumbled into the living room. I was reaching for the phone when I remembered my father had told me never to answer it. Always let the machine take the call.

The machine clicked on.

First there was the sound of somebody clearing his throat. Then the voice began. A deep, raspy voice. Talking in a slow, dreamy way.

"Harry, my friend . . . I've found you, am I right? Where have you been, Harry? Everybody has been asking for you. 'How is Harry?' they say—" He began to cough. Then he cleared his throat. "I'll be coming to visit, Harry," he said. "I could use the fresh air. I would have come sooner, my friend, but nobody had your address."

Then he said slowly, "But now I know where you are." Click. The message ended.

I sat shivering in the dark living room. The strange voice seemed to fill the house, floating like smoke, filling every corner. I couldn't breathe.

I could hear my father snoring.

I didn't dare wake him.

I told him in the morning.

Smoke

The day after Rootie and I had gone to Black-beard's Cove, I was at the ferry landing for the six o'clock boat. There was the usual crowd, nothing to report. I was about to get on my bike.

Then I smelled the cigar smoke. I searched the crowd: Nobody was smoking a cigar. People were carrying bags, suitcases, backpacks. They were holding cameras, books, newspapers, dog leashes, presents, even cigarettes. No cigars.

But the smoke was definitely there. You could

feel it on your skin. I looked around the building where the ticket office was. A few people were already standing in line to go back to the mainland. I checked the cars that were getting in place for the return trip. Still nothing.

Had I missed him? Was he in a taxi, heading for the bungalow?

Should I call my father right away? I pulled out the quarter. My hand was sweating.

What if it was a false alarm?

But what if it wasn't? I could see the taxi now—probably driven by that old man who wore the torn green baseball hat, and who swerved back and forth across the white line—speeding up the hill from the harbor, then turning on Long Pond Road, carrying Looney Tunes in the backseat.

The old man was probably talking to his passenger, telling him stories about the island, and Looney Tunes was probably nodding, not listening at all, as the taxi went down Long Pond to Wampanoag Road.

My father, I guessed, was sitting in the chair by the window, drink in hand, thinking everything was okay—at least for the moment—not knowing that the old taxi was racketing along toward him, closer and closer.

The phone was next to the freight office on the ferry dock, a big shadowy room with forklifts and crates and pallets inside, and usually some guys standing around talking and joking—gnarled old seafaring types and some young summer-job high school or college guys. I ran to the phone, but a woman was using it. "There *are* no taxis," she was saying into the phone. "They're all gone."

I stood near her, tapping my foot, so she would know I was waiting to use the phone.

"Congratulations, man," said a voice from inside the freight office.

"Thanks, buddy," said another voice.

"Awwright! What is it—a boy or girl?"

"Girl. Seven pounds. Have a cigar!"

Cigar smoke was drifting out the door in billows.

"Congratulations, Nick!"

I looked inside. A man was handing out cigars. I put the quarter back in my pocket and leaned against the building.

"I'm through with the phone, young man," said the woman, walking away.

"Thanks," I said. I went to get my bike. I wheeled it over to the far end of the dock and sat down on one of the timbers, letting my feet hang over the edge. I tried to calm down. I was shaking. I watched the dark water swirl around the old pilings. I listened to it gulp under the dock. . . .

"Hey, Pete!"

It was Rootie.

"What are you doing?" she asked.

"Just hanging out," I said.

"Pretty nice day," she said. "I was with Katie and Lila at Ben & Jerry's. They have some weird new flavor."

"Any good?" I said.

"Katie liked it a lot, I thought it was okay but Lila said she was going to barf."

"I guess I'll stick to chocolate raspberry," I said.

"You come down here a lot, don't you?" said Rootie, looking at the ferryboat.

"It's something to do," I said. "I like to see the ferryboat come in. All the people."

"Well, that was the last boat," she said. "What are you going to do now?"

"I don't know. Go home, I guess."

"How long does it take you to get home on your bike?" She was chomping on bubble gum. "Half an hour?"

"Twenty minutes," I said.

"Baloney," she said.

"Twenty-five," I said.

"Half an hour," she said. "I live right where you do, remember? You have to take Harbor Hill Road, and that's a hill, and Long Pond, and Wampanoag—"

"Maybe half an hour," I said.

Rootie made a bubble. *Pop!* Then she said, "I know a shortcut. A secret shortcut. *Ten minutes* from here to home."

"Where is it?" I said.

"Can you keep a secret?" she said, snapping her gum.

"That's what I'm good at," I said.

CHAPTER 6

The Yellow Brick Road

At the top of Harbor Hill Road, Rootie skidded to a stop, her bike sliding around on the sandy pavement. I caught up with her.

She looked up and down the road. There was nobody in sight. "I'll go first," she said in a low voice. "Then, when the coast is clear, you follow me."

"The coast is clear right now," I said.

"Just follow instructions, okay?" said Rootie.

26

"Okay."

She jumped off her bike and ran it across the road. She lifted it over a low place in the old stone wall and disappeared into the woods.

"Come on!" she called.

"In a minute!" I called back.

"Hurry up!" she called.

I waited.

"What's the problem?" she called.

"I'm waiting for the coast to clear."

Rootie peered out of the bushes. "The coast *is* clear," she said.

"Yeah," I said, "but I like it clearer than this."

"Idiot!" she yelled.

A few minutes later we were riding through woods, moving down a narrow dirt path, winding through tall ferns and briars. It was just wide enough for one person, and you had to keep low because the trees twisted down from above. Sometimes you had to shove them away from your face. Rootie was in the lead. I stayed a few yards behind so that the branches she pushed aside wouldn't come lashing back at me. Vines looped down in the tangles, and sharp thorns scratched my legs. You couldn't see the sky at all, and then the trees would break open and the sun would pour down, and then it would close up again.

The path turned swampy, and I smelled skunk. My bike slithered out of control on the mud. "Skunk cabbage!" called Rootie, pointing at the plants on either side—bright green, curling open. A shallow stream crossed the path. Rootie went through it as fast as she could, sending up a wall of water. I rode right into the spray. She looked back and laughed.

Sometimes mossy rocks stuck up from the dirt, and you had to jump them, lifting your front wheel.

Sometimes a branch of poison ivy reached out,

and you'd have to veer fast to miss the shiny leaves.

Sometimes the sweet smell of honeysuckle filled the woods.

Rootie stopped her bike and began poking into some bushes. I came skidding up behind her. "What is it?"

"Blackberries," she said.

I peered into the bushes. Blackberries were everywhere. They looked pretty good.

"Can we eat them?" I said.

"Not yet," she said. "Soon."

She reached over to a bush on the other side of the path and pulled off a couple of leaves. She ground them up in her fingers and stuck out her hand. "Smell," she said.

"Is it a trick?" I said.

"No. It's just a great smell."

I smelled the powdered leaves. "You're right," I said. "What is it?"

"Bayberry," she said. "The best." She smelled it herself. "I love bayberry." Then she dusted off her hands and jumped back on her bike.

We moved on, in and out of the shadows, and then suddenly the woods ended, and we were in a field under the huge sky. Just in front of us was Wampanoag Road.

"Quick, huh?" said Rootie. "I call it the Yellow Brick Road." She pointed to the left. "Your house is over there, and mine is up there. Remember, it's a secret. See you later."

She went across the field, turned right on the road, and disappeared.

CHAPTER 7

The Bronx

I never knew what my father did.

I mean, I never knew what he did for a living.

He was always going someplace in his old green Cadillac, and sometimes he took me with him, especially after my mother was gone.

I liked riding in that car. It had those fuzzy seats—velour, my father said. The floor was fuzzy, too, except in the worn-out places. It was fun to run the electric windows up and down.

"Cut that out, you want to get hurt?" my father would say.

In those days I thought I could never get hurt if my father was around. It couldn't happen.

We would drive to different streets in New York. If he was in a good mood, he'd sing a little.

He would double-park in front of some building. "Watch the car," he'd say, "and don't mess with the windows." Then he'd disappear into the building.

Sometimes it was a long wait, and I got bored. I'd climb into the front seat and grab the steering wheel and pretend to drive. I'd look at the speedometer and imagine I was going ninety miles an hour, a hundred. . . . Once I was fooling around and I found something under the front seat. It was a black club—leather—very heavy. I swung it a couple of times. I hit my hand with it very lightly to see if it hurt. It did.

"What the hell are you doing?" said my father,

opening the door. "Give me that." He grabbed the club.

"I just found it under the seat," I said. "What's it for?"

"It's for people who don't mind their own business," he said. He shoved it under the seat.

I felt like crying.

I bit my lip. After a while my father looked over at me. He could tell I was trying not to cry, I guess.

"Sometimes you have to be ready to defend yourself, you know what I mean?" he said.

"I know," I said. But I didn't really know. I'd been in a couple of fights at school. More like shoving contests. Nobody had a club or anything.

"Better safe than sorry," said my father. "That's what they say."

One cold morning around five, we drove up to the Bronx when it was still dark. The sky was just starting to get a little bit light. We drove into a place where there were cobblestones and lots of trucks lumbering around. It was noisy. The trucks were parking, and starting up, and passing one another. Sometimes, in the headlights, I could see women sort of drifting around on the sidewalks.

"Look at those women," I said. "They're practically naked!"

"I see 'em," he said. "Hookers."

They wore high-heeled shoes or boots, and maybe some little jacket, but that was about all. "They must be freezing," I said.

"Probably are," said my father.

I had my nose pressed against the window, I guess. I'd never seen a real live naked woman before. I'd seen pictures, like in the *Playboy* magazines Herbie had hidden in his basement, but never anybody walking around like this. The window fogged up, and I had to wipe it clear. "Don't stare," said my father.

He parked by the entrance to a huge garage. "I'll be right back," he said. He walked into the garage. It was full of enormous garbage trucks. I lost sight of him. The trucks were moving in and out, backing up, beeping, gears grinding; trucks were driving away.

"Hi," said a woman's voice. I jumped. It was one of the women from the sidewalk. She was standing by the car, hugging herself and shivering. "You're up early," she said.

I didn't know what to say. She was good-looking, I thought. Should I say, "Are you cold?" That would be dumb. So I didn't say anything.

"At least you could say hello," she said.

"Hello," I said.

She laughed. "How old are you?"

"Nine," I said.

"I have a little boy who's six," she said. "When's your birthday?"

"May," I said.

"He's October," she said. "October third."

She must have heard something then, something I didn't hear, because she swung around suddenly and looked toward the entrance to the garage. I stared at her bare rear end without meaning to. I couldn't help it. And then she was running away down the street, teetering on her high heels, and when I looked back toward the garage I saw what had startled her.

It was my father, coming out of the garage backward, his arms up, his coat flying as two men took turns hitting him. With each punch, I could see a fine spray of blood against the lights of the garage. They gave him a final shove, and he came reeling toward the car. There was blood all over his face and on his clothes.

By the time I got the club out from under the

seat, he was in the car, slumped over, dripping from his chin onto the steering wheel and down to the velour.

The brown blood stains never came out no matter what, but we didn't have the Cadillac much longer, anyway. By then we were on the run.

The Hyperion

You wouldn't know it had been a movie theater, seeing it from the outside. It didn't look like one of those fancy old movie places, and it didn't look like a Cinema 1–2–3–4, either. It was just a low, ramshackle building standing between a bike rental and the drugstore. Plywood had been nailed over the doors and windows, and it just seemed like a plain old building that was abandoned and forgotten. Maybe a hardware store once. Maybe a grocery. But the years of rain and sleet and snow had scrubbed off any color it used to have, and now it was just a blurry memory, standing in the weeds, and people walked by with their ice-cream cones and never gave it a second thought.

Rootie knew what it was, of course. We had stopped our bikes in front of it. "Look over the door," she said. "Can you read that?"

I didn't see anything at first. Then I began to make out the letters. H . . . Y . . . P . . . then a B, or an E . . .

"H . . . Y . . P . . . E . . . R . . . I . . . O . . . N," said Rootie.

"What does it mean?"

"It's a name they used to give to theaters. Like Criterion or Lyceum. I saw a book in the library."

"This was a movie theater?"

"You got it," said Rootie. "Want to go inside?"

"How could you do that?" I said.

Rootie glanced around. "Wait a sec," she said.

A tall, skinny kid in baggy shorts was walking across the street toward us.

"Hey, Rootie," he said in a drawly voice.

"Hey, Tim," she said.

"What are you doing?" he said, scratching his neck and staring at me.

"The usual," said Rootie. "Nothing."

He grinned and stretched. "I know what you mean," he said. "This place is bor-ring. All my friends have gone to the Vineyard." He walked away.

"Who's that?" I asked.

"A dork," said Rootie. "He comes every summer—after they let him out of summer school."

She watched the cars and mopeds for a minute. Then she said, "This way," and ran her bike down the alley between the theater and the drugstore.

At the back of the theater she put her bike in

some tall weeds. I put my bike next to hers, and by the time I turned around she was crawling under the building. The floor was about three feet off the ground, held up by old beams that sat on wooden posts or stacks of rocks. Nothing looked very solid or strong. Everything was tilted one way or another. I crawled after her. It was damp, and you had to watch out for broken glass.

Rootie reached up and pushed a piece of plywood aside. Then she hoisted herself up.

I followed her.

"How do you like it?" said Rootie.

The theater was a big, dim room with a stage and a stained old screen with rips in it and rows of seats—a lot of them broken. Trash was strewn all around: pieces of cardboard, movie posters, popcorn boxes, beer bottles. Light streamed in through the cracks between the boards of the walls, catching the dust and cobwebs.

"I like it," I said.

Rootie plunked herself down in one of the seats. She turned around and looked up at the projection booth at the back of the orchestra. "Start the movie!" she called. Then she settled down, putting her feet on top of the seat in front of her. "We should have brought popcorn," she said.

Flap-flap. A pigeon took off from one of the beams overhead, flew around, and settled on a different beam.

"If I owned this place," said Rootie, "I'd let kids in free. If they were quiet. No bullies. No yelling or running around or kicking the seats. I'd show all the movies I like. My favorites."

"What movie first?"

"*The Wizard of Oz.* That's a great movie."

"Yeah, it is."

"That's why I named the secret path the Yellow Brick Road."

"I like the Wicked Witch of the West and the Munchkins."

"I like the shoes sticking out from under the house."

"I like the straw man and the tin man and the cowardly lion," I said.

"Me, too," said Rootie. "If you had to pick, which would you want the most—a heart or a brain or courage?"

"I don't know," I said. I knew, but I didn't want to tell her.

Courage.

"The last time I saw *The Wizard of Oz* was when my parents were fighting all the time, starting to get a divorce," said Rootie. "The movie scared me a lot. Especially the part at the beginning when the twister comes and picks up the house and starts whirling it up into the sky. It was just like what was happening in my own house." She unwrapped a piece of bubble gum. "Want some?"

"No thanks," I said.

She chewed for a while. "I just shut my eyes and held my ears and waited for that part to be over. Every so often I'd take a peek, but the house was still spinning or the cackling woman was going by on her bike with Toto in the basket, so I'd shut my eyes again, as tight as I could. Then finally I opened my eyes and everything in the movie was in color, and there were flowers all over the place, and it was warm and sunny, and everybody was nice. I loved that."

"Is that why you stay at your grandmother's?" I asked. "Because your parents are divorced?"

"Yeah, sort of," said Rootie. "I mean, that way it's a lot easier. Last winter I lived at her apartment in New York. It's cool. No parents stressed out, or saying bad things about the other one all the time. No new sleazy girlfriends or boyfriends you have to be nice to. It's like time out. My grandmother is probably the person I like the best of anybody."

"Did she give you that fancy bike?" I said.

"No, my father did. That's what happens when your parents get divorced. You get good presents. They're competing with each other."

"To show how much they care about you?"

"That, and to make the other one look bad." She popped her gum. "Either way, you get good presents. Are your parents divorced?"

"No, not really," I said.

"What does that mean?"

"Well, my mother is in a hospital. She's been there a long time," I said.

"Is it like cancer or something?" said Rootie.

"No, it's mental. She used to get depressed a lot, and it got worse, and then she just kind of drifted away in her mind, and they don't know how to bring her back."

"Do you ever see her?" asked Rootie.

"A couple of years ago was the last time. I don't like to talk about it much."

"You must feel awful. Sorry."

"That's okay," I said.

"How does your father take it? Is he all right?"

"I don't know," I said. "He drinks. A lot."

"All the time, you mean?"

"Most of it," I said.

"You can't do anything about that, I guess."

"No, I can't," I said. "I think maybe he wants to kill himself. One way or another. Fast or slow."

"Has he tried?" said Rootie.

"I don't exactly know. He has a handgun—a .38 Special—and it's supposed to be for protection. But one day I saw him sitting in the window where he usually sits, and he was holding the gun. He didn't know I was around. I was riding my bike across the lawn to the porch, and I looked through the window and he was putting the gun up to his head. Slowly, like an experiment. Then he held it there, and I was sure he was going to pull the trigger."

"What did you do?" said Rootie.

"I jumped off my bike and threw it down on the porch steps, so it made a big noise. Then I walked up the steps as if I hadn't seen him. I was really scared. When I finally looked at him, he had put the gun down. He looked like he didn't want to be caught. It was weird—him pretending he didn't do it, and me pretending I hadn't seen him. And after that, all that day and night, I kept waiting to see if he was going to try again. Any minute it might happen."

"What could you do?" said Rootie.

"Well, the next day, when my father was in the yard, I went to the table where he kept the gun, and I took it out of the drawer. I went down into the cellar, and I hid the gun under the cellar stairs. I covered it with an old bag of grass seed. Later on, when he discovered the gun was gone, we had a big argument. He accused me of taking it, but I said I didn't take it, he must have lost it. I said maybe he forgot where he'd put it. That made him really mad. Because it was so close to the truth. When he drinks, he has blackouts a lot, and he can't remember what he did or didn't do."

"That was a good idea, hiding the gun," said Rootie.

I didn't tell her the rest of the idea, which was if one day Looney Tunes got off the boat I'd call my father and tell him where I had hidden the gun, so my father could get it and be ready.

"Hey," I said. "I don't want to talk about this stuff anymore."

"We can talk about something else," said Rootie. "What do you want to talk about?"

"How come you don't tell me where you got the name Rootie?"

"I will tell you," said Rootie. "I don't mind."

"So?"

"My grandmother gave it to me. She says there was an old comic-strip character named Rootie Kazootie, or something like that. The character must have been always racing around or maybe looked like me. You could ask her. Anyway, she started calling me Rootie Kazootie, and then it got shortened to Rootie."

"What's your real name?"

"Rosalie Ann Bowditch," she said. "Go ahead. Laugh."

"That's not a bad name."

"At school they used to call me Dowbitch," said Rootie. "That's what kids like to do."

"Well, I like Rootie better anyway."

"Me, too." *Pop.*

Mother

I asked my father about my mother one day after she'd been gone a long time. I didn't want to ask, but I kept wondering where she was and what she was doing. I wondered why she had left us, left all of a sudden.

I used to dream about her all the time, that she had come home, or maybe she had never left, and in the dream she was in the kitchen, at the stove, stirring something, and it was like when I was a little kid, hanging out in the kitchen, watching her cook, knowing supper was going to come along. But in the dream, when my mother turned toward me, her eyes were blank and her face was blank, and she didn't ever hear my voice. It was like a person miles and miles away, across a huge valley, and she couldn't hear me calling, and I called louder and louder and louder, but it did no good. I'd wake up from the dream in a cold sweat, sometimes with my hands on the wall, fumbling in the dark to try to find the door, trying to get out of the room, trying to escape the darkness, and the dream.

When I asked my father about my mother, he said maybe we could go see her, she was in a hospital, he'd find out. Then one day he said, "Today we're going to go and see your mother." I made her a card that said, "I love you. Get well soon." We got in the car and drove a long way.

"She may not say anything to you," he said. "She doesn't talk much at all, the doctor said. But she'll be glad to see you, I know that."

At last we went through big gates and up a winding driveway with black trees along it, and then I saw old brown buildings from long ago with weird roofs and spires and stone porches, and in some of the windows I saw bars. It was sad and scary, and between the buildings were concrete sidewalks and every so often a park bench with nobody on it.

We went inside one of the buildings, and my father talked to a doctor. Then a man in a white coat took us down a long hall that had a tan linoleum floor. We came to a door. We waited while the man pulled out some keys from his pocket and unlocked the door, and there was another long hall, and the man locked the door behind us. We walked and walked past rooms with people sitting in them—I didn't want to stare at them, but I was scared, just seeing some of the faces looking out as we went by.

"Sharon?" said the man. "You have some visitors." Then he turned to us and said quietly, "She gets tired quickly." We went into the room.

My mother was in a bathrobe, sitting in a chair, slumped forward, staring straight ahead.

"Hello, Sharon," said my father, very quietly. "I brought Pete to see you," he said. She didn't move.

"Give her a kiss, Pete," said my father.

"Hi, Mom," I said, and kissed her cheek. Slowly, slowly, she turned her head toward me. Her face was as blank as in the dream, but it was worse because this wasn't a dream. "Are you okay?" I asked. "I miss you, Mom." I gave her the card, but she just let it dangle from her fingers. She gazed at my father, then looked straight ahead again. She was wearing blue furry slippers.

"Maybe Sharon would like to go for a little walk," said the man in the doorway.

She didn't answer. We sat in the room for a long time. Sometimes my father would say something like, "Pete's doing well in his school," but it floated in the air, never any answer, and after a while we got up to go. We said good-bye and kissed her again. She didn't say a word, and then we went down the hall, and the man unlocked the door. We walked down the tan linoleum hallway and went home. I never made her a card after that.

The Storm

The first week of July the whole world turned green—a color of sky I'd never seen before—and there was a strange calm. Then a soft, warm wind came along, whispering warnings you couldn't quite figure out.

But the island people understood; they'd heard it on the radio. The storm was moving up the coast, eighty mile-an-hour winds, twelve-foot waves.

Rootie and I rode through town, watching the people get ready. At the rental place, guys were wheeling bikes and mopeds indoors as fast as they could. We heard hammering, and as we turned onto Bay Street we saw store owners nailing plywood over their windows. On the beach next to the harbor, guys were carrying surfboards two at a time into the shack, while others hauled Sunfish and sailboards high up toward the dunes. A line of boats—yachts, lobster boats, Boston Whalers, fishing boats, ocean racers, outboards, cigarette boats—were all coming in from the sea, going past the point, and into the shelter of Teach's Bay with its docks and marinas.

We sped down the slope to the ferry dock across the empty parking lot. At the ticket office the windows were closed.

NO FERRIES UNTIL FURTHER NOTICE, said a sign, DUE TO WEATHER.

When I read the sign, I let out a yelp. Rootie

looked at me and laughed. She didn't know what the yelp meant.

But I was free.

No boats to watch. Nobody could come to the island. Absolutely nobody, as long as the storm continued.

I rode my bike in loopy circles across the white lines of the parking lot. Rootie jumped on her bike, and we played follow the leader, zooming around the ticket office, the freight office, the pay phone, over to the harbormaster's shack, around that and out onto a narrow dock and back. We circled a mountain of lobster pots, veered in and out of a line of no-parking signs, went bouncing up and down the steps of Rabson's Seafood Restaurant (closed) at the far end of the harbor, and then raced each other at top speed all the way back to Bay Street, where we skidded to a stop (Rootie won by maybe three feet), dropped our bikes, plunked ourselves down on one of the benches, and sat there gasping as the cars and people hurried by, heading for shelter.

It wasn't long before things changed. The sky darkened, clouds churning, boiling, tumbling— and the wind picked up, shrieking around the buildings, thrumming the telephone wires, slamming doors. At the antique store the swinging sign whipped back and forth, screeching on its old hinges. Plastic trash cans were bounding across Bay Street, heading for the beach, spraying papers like confetti.

A police car with lights flashing cruised by. It stopped just past us and backed up. The old cop cupped his hand to yell at us. "You kids—go home right now! Do you need a ride?"

We shook our heads no.

"Well, hurry up," he called. "This thing is moving in fast!" He drove on, and we got back on our bikes.

It was hard to pedal. The wind shoved us sideways. But after we turned the corner by the Harbor Hotel, where the empty rocking chairs were seesawing on the porch, the wind was behind us and we went sailing down the street, no need to pedal now, our legs stuck out sideways, flying.

At the Quality Food Market, past the gift shop and Nick's Pizza, people were getting last-minute supplies, running bent over like crabs, hugging brown paper bags, scuttling toward their cars. But the wind grabbed the people and pushed them so they did a kind of dance—one step forward, two steps back—and when they finally got into their cars, they had to struggle to get the doors closed. We watched a man in a yellow slicker and rain hat lurching across the parking lot. A gust of wind grabbed his hat and tore it off his head. The hat went soaring up over the roof of the market and joined a flock of seagulls, a yellow speck in the crowd of white.

We went up the hill—we had to push our bikes

now—and took the Yellow Brick Road home. It was more sheltered along the path, but overhead the branches were lashing wildly, making lots of noise. When we came out into the field, we felt the first raindrops—one here, one there, now another—and we ran through the grass yelling because it felt so great, the warm rain coming down, and by the time we reached Wampanoag Road it was a downpour, with rivers streaming along the sides of the road where there had only been grass and goldenrod.

That night the power went off—at 2:47, according to the clocks that stopped—and it stayed off for two days. Winds ripped trees from the ground and sent them sprawling across the roads. Hail hit the window like buckshot. Lawns turned into lakes. The rain took over the empty roads, traveling in waves down to the ponds, filling them until the bridges themselves were half-submerged.

Practically nobody went out except maybe to grab an armload of firewood or to check on their boats.

For two days, for Rootie and me, the island was ours. Rootie's grandmother said I could stay at her house during the storm. I asked my father. He didn't care.

Mrs. Bowditch's house was big and yellow with wide porches. On one side were gardens. It was an old house with rooms that smelled as if the air had stayed in there a long time, and pictures so faded you couldn't tell what they were supposed to be. The chairs and sofas were worn out, kind of collapsing but still okay, and the floors were warped and creaky, and slanted in different directions. I liked the house a lot. It seemed like a place where people could spend their whole lives, beginning to end, and nothing would change.

They gave me a room that had a great view

across the meadow to the ocean. Sometimes, when I was cold from running around in the rain with Rootie, I'd wrap myself in an old blanket that smelled of mothballs and watch the ocean through the wobbly windowpanes. It looked like some monstrous green creature rising up on its hind legs, twisting and writhing, trying to reach people on the land.

But I felt safe inside the old yellow house.

Rootie's grandmother warned us not to touch fallen wires, which we knew already, and to be home before it got dark, which was okay, too, and then we set off to explore and see all the changes. We kept an eye out for the police, and if we spotted a cruiser, we ducked for cover.

We ran everywhere in bare feet, and when our clothes got too sodden we went home and changed, ate a peanut butter sandwich maybe, and then set out again.

Once, when the wind and rain got too savage, we crawled under the front porch of the Bayview Hotel and crouched there, watching the waterfall pour from the edge of the porch, cutting us off the from the outside world, protecting us.

At Far Beach we slithered under an upturned dory and listened to the drumming on the hull over our heads. When the rain let up a little, we ran down the beach, jumping over heaps of seaweed, looking for whatever stuff the sea might have delivered. The waves towered like mountains, and the wind ripped the foam from their peaks, whirling it into snowstorms that flew around us.

We found an open window at the back of the Midnight Hour, the nightclub between Super Sub and Son of the Beach Men's Fashions. We climbed in, knocking over empty bottles, and sat in one of the booths with slippery vinyl seats.

When we got used to the dark, we saw the low stage with its speakers and amps and standing mikes.

Rootie jumped up, grabbed a mike, and began singing a song about going to a chapel and getting married, and doing dances she had learned from her mother, like the Locomotion and the Monkey. It was pretty funny. Especially because she looked so serious when she did it.

That was one of the good things about Rootie. She didn't make fun of whatever it was; she did it the best she could. I didn't like it when kids or grown-ups twisted a word, say, to let you know they were better or smarter than whatever they were saying. I liked it when people said what they meant and just went ahead and did it.

"And now, ladies and gentlemen," said Rootie, holding the mike, "we have the great privilege of introducing the one and only, now touring

his Top 40 hit, the ever-popular Mr. Music himself . . . Pete!"

I sang an old Coasters song called "Yakety
Yak" that Herbie had on tape, and Rootie
clapped. Then she held up her hands as if to
quiet the audience. "Please! Please! Quiet,
please. Everybody please go home . . . Mr. Pete
has now left the building."

That broke me up.

I guess it was a little while after we finished
singing that we were just talking, and Rootie told
me more about her mother and father, stuff she
hadn't ever told anybody else.

I thought about how we were sort of alike,
both of us carrying around all these things we
couldn't tell anybody else.

When Rootie had finished talking, we sat in
the booth for a while, not saying anything. I
began to feel it was definitely my turn now.

But I kept thinking about my father, and how I wasn't supposed to say anything to anybody, ever.

Rootie sat there, waiting. Probably wondering why I wouldn't be as honest as she had been. Feeling this wasn't going to be a real friendship after all. Feeling she'd made a mistake taking a chance with me.

It must have seemed to her like I had betrayed her. I could feel Rootie pulling away, taking back her feelings, covering up. It was like watching somebody leave. Walking away, getting smaller and smaller.

She had trusted me.

Now I had to trust her.

I told Rootie everything.

I told her about my parents. I told her how, when I was younger, I guess I had thought my mother and father would take care of me. If things went wrong, they'd protect me. Well, that wasn't the way it went, because pretty soon my mother began to get sick, and then she was gone, and my father was drinking all the time, and in a rage, violent.

I remembered Pennsylvania—some little town in the mountains. My father and I were traveling all the time then, a different place almost every night, and we ended up in this dinky town. It had a courthouse and, across the street, an old hotel. The main street was about four blocks long, I guess, and most of the stores had gone out of business. It seemed like everybody had left the town and moved away.

It was winter, and there was a lot of dirty snow piled up, and a clammy mist wrapped around the mountains. The hotel was mostly empty. It had a lobby with broken tiles on the floor, and a sick-looking palm tree drooping in the corner.

There was nothing to do, nowhere to go, nothing to see. I tried walking down a couple of side streets, but it was all the same: icy sidewalks, frozen laundry on clotheslines, and mean-looking dogs in backyards, barking their heads off.

My father stayed in our room all day, with the TV going. He didn't watch it. He just had it on. And he drank.

I walked to the end of the main street, looking for a place that maybe would have chewing gum. No luck. I was passing this old gas station—it was closed, of course—but I saw a pay phone next to it. There was snow piled up around it. I guess nobody ever used the phone.

I had an idea.

I would call my old friend Herbie.

Collect.

If Herbie was home, he'd accept the call. If his parents answered, they probably wouldn't. But there was a chance Herbie would be the one.

My father had told me plenty of times: Never call anybody on the phone. Ever. *Ever*.

But this time, standing in this place a million miles from nowhere, I was desperate to speak to somebody. I had to hear a voice, maybe a voice like Herbie's that would even say my name, and ask how was I doing, and what's new, and stuff like that.

I looked both ways up and down the street. There was only a delivery truck with a guy lifting some package out of the back, and one old guy shuffling down the sidewalk with a cane.

I climbed up onto the snowbank.

I put the cold receiver to my ear, and pushed the O for operator. The phone rang and rang. Nothing happened. Finally the operator came on, and I said I wanted to make a collect call. I knew Herbie's number by heart. I told her my name.

There was another long wait. Then I could hear the phone ringing. I started to laugh. I was so excited.

On about the fifth ring somebody picked up the phone.

Let it be Herbie, I said to myself. *Please!*

"Hello," said Herbie.

"Herbie!" I yelled. "It's me!"

"One moment, please," said the operator. "Will you accept a collect call from Pete?"

"Say yes, Herbie!" I said.

"Sure," said Herbie.

"Go ahead," said the operator.

The receiver was jerked out of my hand, and I was suddenly yanked backward off the snow-bank and thrown onto the pavement. I looked up, and there was my father.

His face was almost purple. He started kicking at me. "Get up!" he yelled. "Get up!"

As soon as I could get to my feet, he gave me a shove, and I fell down again. He kicked me some more. I got up and started to run, but he was right behind me, smacking the back of my head. "What's the matter with you—you trying to get me killed?" he roared. "I oughta kill *you*!" He hit me on my back, and I slipped on the ice and fell again, and what I remember is spinning downward, and seeing the courthouse, and then the hotel, and then the courthouse again.

I remembered every single time in my life that my father hit me. I remembered exactly where we were, and what was said, and the look on his face, and his arm coming around and the whack of his hand on my face.

I couldn't forget, no matter how hard I tried, and that's why, sometimes, I hoped—for a minute, anyway—that they would send the man soon to kill my father. And if I saw that man coming, maybe I wouldn't warn my father at all.

I would just be quiet.

Quiet.

Quiet.

What Rootie said later, when I had finished, made me feel really good. She didn't say anything drippy. All she said was, "I could help, you know? I could help you watch the boats."

So when the morning came, a day later, the morning that everybody was waiting for, when the sun rose on a fresh, clear day with a light blue sky and puffy clouds and a sparkling sea, and steam rose from the wet shingles of the houses, and people went walking down the streets, calling to each other happily—the day that I had hoped somehow, some way, would never come, the day the ferryboats began again—it wasn't so bad, not as bad as I thought, because now I wasn't all by myself anymore.

CHAPTER 11

Mrs. Bowditch

It was a few days later that Rootie and I started building the tree house.

We picked a tree with a lot of branches—Rootie said it was a beech tree—that stood in the woods about twenty yards behind the house. There was a place on the trunk, maybe twelve feet above the ground, where three or four branches grew outward, kind of flat. That looked like a perfect spot for a tree house. Rootie and I climbed up and stood on the gray branches. The leaves were thick, which was good; it meant people wouldn't see the tree house unless they were almost right under it. But we could see out in different directions. We could see the road and the house and even some ocean across the field.

"Right here," said Rootie. "This is the place to build it. What do you think?"

"This is it," I said. We climbed down, and that afternoon the work began.

Rootie and I rode our bikes to the island dump after it closed for the day. Nobody was around, just a bunch of seagulls squawking. We put our bikes near big bins of broken bottles—brown, white, green. The glass sparkled like jewels in giant pirate trunks. It was a scorcher of a day, and the heat cooked the garbage, sending up a stench so strong you could hardly breathe. But after a while you just got used to it.

We walked past big trailers with piles of old cinder blocks, sinks, toilets, bricks, scraps of lumber. On the bluff above the ocean, a dozen sad-looking rusty trucks—pickups, vans, flatbeds, a bakery truck, delivery trucks, a faded old fire engine—were sunk in the tall grass, their hoods open as if they'd died gasping for air. Curly vines crawled through the busted windshields. Beyond the trucks, the ocean waves came roaring in, throwing gray foam like spit on the old dead trucks.

In an hour Rootie and I collected sheets of plywood, two-by-fours, pieces of heavy rope. By the time we'd carried everything we needed back to the beech tree, Rootie and I were in a sweat.

"Let's go to White Shark Beach and grab a swim," said Rootie.

"White Shark Beach?" I said.

"White Shark Beach," said Rootie.

"Why don't we just cool off right here?" I said. "I'm pretty tired." I started to sit down.

"You are?" said Rootie. "I'm not."

"Where is this White Shark Beach anyway?" I said.

"Just past my house," she said. "Want to see it?"

"Someday," I said.

"It usually has pretty good waves."

I didn't say anything.

"You don't mind white sharks, do you?" said Rootie. "They don't come in very often."

"I guess I don't mind them any more than you do," I said.

In a minute we were on our bikes, heading for the beach. Rootie began humming the music from *Jaws*—the dum-dum dum-dum *dum-dum* theme.

"Knock it off," I said.

Ten minutes later we were on a low bluff, looking at a small, perfect beach. Rootie ran down and across the beach and made a crazy dive into the waves.

"Come on!" she yelled when she came up in the water. "It's cool!"

I looked past her for fins that might be slicing through the water. I couldn't be sure, but I thought I saw three or four.

"Hurry up!" called Rootie.

I went down the face of the bluff and stood at the edge of the water. The waves swirled around my ankles. Rootie floated around a few yards out, grinning.

Got to do it, I said to myself. Got to.

I ran in, dove under a wave, and then I was swimming along in green water, a few inches above the smooth sand, holding my breath. When I couldn't hold it any longer, I came up, and I was face to face with a tall wave about to break. I took a deep breath and plunged under again, and I could feel the shudder of the wave passing overhead.

"Is there some story about this beach?" I said to Rootie when I came up. "I mean, when did it get named White Shark Beach?"

Rootie looked thoughtful. Then she said, "About twenty minutes ago" and started to laugh.

"Thanks," I said.

"It's really called Little Bay Beach," said Rootie. "But that's *so* boring."

We swam for a long time, and it was really fun, and then we climbed the bluff and headed across the meadow to Mrs. Bowditch's house.

Mrs. Bowditch was in her garden, where she usually was, crawling around, yanking up weeds, tossing them into a basket, digging with a trowel.

"Hello, dearies!" she said. "How was the water?"

We said it was great.

"Take some towels and dry off," she said.

"I'll get them," said Rootie, and went inside.

I sat down on the warm steps of the porch.

Mrs. Bowditch wore dirty gloves, a blue work shirt, jeans, and ratty sneakers that once might have been white. She took off her hat—a torn straw hat that might have been run over by a truck—and wiped her forehead with her glove, leaving a streak of mud. "Hot as Hades, isn't it?" she said. Her hair was white, a crazy tangle. She was maybe seventy-five—Rootie didn't know exactly—and she looked like a hawk: sharp-eyed and tough. She was skinny, all bones, and probably weighed about ninety pounds.

Mrs. Bowditch reached into the pocket of her jeans, then called out in a raspy voice, "Damn it,

Rootie—I forgot my ciggies! Be a dear? They're probably by the sink."

"Okay," called Rootie from inside the house.

Around four o'clock most afternoons, when long shadows began moving across the garden, Mrs. Bowditch got to her feet slowly and stiffly, picked up her basket of weeds and trowel and clippers, and went up the porch steps, clutching the railing, into the house. Twenty minutes later she would come out, wearing a frayed white bathrobe, a towel around her neck, and a rubber bathing cap on top of her head, and she would walk across the lawn to the beach for her afternoon swim.

When she came back, she would peel off her bathing cap—it made a glopping sound—and shake her white hair. "The water was blissful," she'd say, and go into the house.

Pretty soon there would be the sound of music from the living room (Mrs. Bowditch had a stack

of fat old records, and a record player) and her
favorite was a big band song called "Begin The
Beguine."

By then she would be all dressed up, and she'd
dance around while she made a drink she called
"a very, very dry martini" in a cocktail shaker—
sort of like what milkshakes are made in, but this
was silver, and full of ice rattling.

"What's a beguine?" asked Rootie one afternoon.

"Why, it's a dance," said Mrs. Bowditch. "You
know, like a samba, or a rumba, or a fox-trot?"

We both shook our heads. No.

"Fred Astaire?" she said, twisting a sliver of
lemon over her drink. "Ginger Rogers?"

We shook our heads again.

Then Mrs. Bowditch would start telling us
about when she was young, and all the dances
she would go to, and "stag lines," and "debs,"
and the nightclubs where she went when she was

only fifteen. We heard about swizzle sticks, and the Stork Club, and LaRue, Eddie Condon's. Sometimes she talked about trips to Europe on big ocean liners, or fishing in the Adirondacks, or shooting birds—"Birds?" said Rootie. "Like robins? Bluebirds?"

"Like grouse," said Mrs. Bowditch. "Like quail."

Sometimes she talked about a ranch out west with real cowboys, and going on pack trips into the mountains, or rafting down dangerous rapids. The stories went on and on, winding here and there, and we hardly ever knew the things she was talking about, because it was all a long time ago, and all gone.

Around five-thirty I always had to leave so I could watch the six o'clock boat come in. "I better go home now," I'd say. Probably Mrs. Bowditch wondered why; maybe Rootie told her some reason.

So I'd jump on my bike and go down to the ferryboat, watch the people get off, and then ride back to my house. My father would be sitting by the window, watching the road. You couldn't see him, but I knew he was there. And I knew he'd have his glass of vodka in his hand, poured straight from the bottle. No lemon. Not even any ice.

The Tree House

The tree house we built over the next couple of days was made of a platform that rested on two-by-fours tied to the branches. We nailed sticks to the trunk, each one about a foot above the other, making a ladder from the ground straight up to the platform. We put the steps on the far side of the tree trunk, so people passing by couldn't see them. The platform itself was almost invisible because of the leaves. Nobody would think to look up there anyway.

We named the tree house The Ship, and we spied on the cars going by. Sometimes Rootie and I pretended that we were buccaneers hiding from the British navy. Sometimes we fired cannons at the other ships. Sometimes we just hung out, lying flat on the warm plywood deck, feeling the sun coming through the leaves above, watching the whitecaps on the ocean.

I liked being there with Rootie. It was peaceful, like being on a real ship with a good breeze, sailing away to where nobody could ever reach us.

Then sometimes, suddenly, I'd hear my father crashing around in the house, cursing, a glass breaking—and our voyage was over. Our ship had hit a reef, and we were just one more shipwreck.

CHAPTER 13

Salt Water Taffy

"That could be him," said Rootie suddenly, grabbing my arm. "Look!"

We were standing to one side of the dock where the cars were coming off the ten o'clock boat. It was a Saturday morning, and lots of people were streaming past us. I couldn't see right away who Rootie had spotted. "Where?" I said.

"On the stairs," she said. She pointed, keeping her elbow by her side so nobody would notice she was pointing.

Then I saw him.

Tall, heavy, wearing an old-fashioned gray hat and dark glasses. Suit and tie. A shopping bag hanging from one hand.

He paused halfway down the stairs of the ferry and looked out over the island, his dark glasses catching the light as he looked slowly this way and that.

It was a careful look, the look of somebody who didn't know the place, had never been there before. Taking it all in.

Then he continued down the stairs. His suit was a rumpled blue suit, and his shoes were black, shoes probably used to sidewalks and subways. There was nothing about him that would make you think sightseer.

"Under his coat," said Rootie. "He's holding something under his coat."

Rootie was right. He had something bulky inside his coat.

"Could be a nine-millimeter," said Rootie.

"How do you know that?" I said.

"I know plenty," she said. "Maybe a .357 Magnum. In a shoulder holster."

I started to shake. I couldn't help it. I should be calling my father. One more minute. Just to make sure. Then I'd run to the phone.

He walked off the ferry and stood on the dock, looking around.

Then he put down the shopping bag, reached into his breast pocket, and pulled out a cigar.

"It's him," I said to Rootie. My voice was quivering. "It's really him."

The man unwrapped the cigar, bit off the end, spat it out on the concrete, and lit the cigar with a lighter—all the time holding his other arm close to his side, holding the bulky object.

"Better call," said Rootie. Her voice was shaking, too.

The smoke was drifting across the dock. I could smell it. I felt sick.

The man stood gazing at the street above the dock, smoke curling around him. His mouth was turned down, and now I could see that he was angry, maybe always angry.

I took the quarter out of my pocket.

"I'm going to call," I said to Rootie. "You stay here. Watch where he goes—"

"Martin! Martin!" A woman's voice cut through the air.

The man turned. "Where the hell have you been?" he said, taking the cigar out of his mouth.

"Traffic!" said the woman. "So much traffic here!" She was about his age, dressed in shorts and a Cutlass Island T-shirt, hauling two small children. "Daddy! Daddy!" they cried.

The man took off his hat—he was bald as an egg—and gave his wife a hug. "How's it going?

Everybody enjoying themselves? Do you like the house?"

They all talked at once, telling him how great everything was. "Wait till you see the beach!" "We rented bikes!" Stuff like that. And then the man reached into his coat and pulled out the bulky object—a brightly colored box. "Salt water taffy!" he said. "Who likes salt water taffy?" They all squealed.

Rootie and I turned away. I put the quarter back in my pocket, and we walked over to where we'd left our bikes. Then we just sat down on the sand and stared at the sea, not even talking. Just worn out.

CHAPTER 1 4

The Attic

One rainy afternoon we were telling Mrs. Bowditch about The Ship.

"We still need some more stuff," said Rootie.
"Like a sail."

"Grog," said Mrs. Bowditch. "Hardtack."

"Exactly," said Rootie. "Ship's stores."

"Why don't you look in the attic?" said Mrs.
Bowditch.

She led us up a dark narrow staircase off the

kitchen to the second floor, then up another stair that led to an attic the size of a cavern. It was dusty and dim, full of suitcases and trunks and boxes and china and furniture and books and pictures. Across the rafters were fishing rods and oars and beach umbrellas and rolled-up rugs.

"Help yourself," said Mrs. Bowditch. She sat down on an old brown trunk that was covered with faded stickers—names of hotels and ships from long ago—and lit a cigarette.

We didn't even know where to start. We opened boxes. Sometimes it was clothes—a velvet bag, a hat—sometimes old letters, sometimes photographs in brown albums that were split and peeling. The pages of the albums were black paper, and the names of the people in the pictures, and the dates, like 1926, were written in white ink. Somebody had taken the trouble to write in all those names and dates so people would know who they were and where and when—but by now, I figured, nobody knew those names any-way.

The rain was coming down hard on the roof over our heads.

Rootie was dressing up in old costumes now, wearing necklaces and straw hats and long dresses, adding different things, like the big old cowboy hat or a cape, or carrying a parasol.

"How do I look?" Rootie would say.

"You look terribly attractive," Mrs. Bowditch would say, and we'd all laugh.

We finally decided on a small square leather trunk. "It looks like a pirate trunk, don't you think?" said Rootie.

"Probably was," said Mrs. Bowditch. "God knows."

We carried it downstairs to the kitchen. "Now we fill it with grog and rations," said Rootie.

Then I saw the clock on the kitchen wall. 6:42.

I'd missed the six o'clock boat.

I said I had to go, and went out into the rain, and jumped on my bike. The wheels slipped on the wet grass, and then I was racing down the road, through the puddles, squinting against the downpour, pedaling as fast I could.

It wasn't the first boat I'd missed. There'd been one in May, and two more in June, but that was all. Three boats.

I veered around a bend in the road, and as soon as I saw my house—almost the very same minute—I smelled the cigar smoke, hanging in the rain.

Visitor

I got off my bike and crept over to a maple tree that had a good view of the house.

I peeked around the trunk. They were in the living room, facing each other, my father and Looney Tunes.

My father was slumped in his chair, and Looney Tunes—a big slobby-looking guy—was sitting on the sofa, one arm over the back, with the fat bulging out. He wore dark glasses, and he had a cigar in his mouth. On his head was a plaid hat. He looked like a man who had just stepped out of the rain for a minute.

One old guy having a visit with another old guy.

Except when Looney Tunes waved his hand. Then you could see he was holding a gun. It wasn't like my father's. It was an automatic. Probably a nine-millimeter.

Over my head the rain was pouring off the maple tree and going down the back of my neck. I wished I had a windbreaker with a collar I could turn up. Or a baseball hat. I wished I had one of those yellow slickers with a hood.

Then I thought, What's the matter with you? What is your problem? How can you be worrying about your wet shirt when your father could be getting killed any second?

I had to try to save his life. I had a chance, if I acted fast.

But what could I do?

Maybe get on my bike and go back to Rootie's house and call the police.

No good. By the time I got halfway there, Looney would have shot my father, and it would be all over.

Or I could sneak into the house and get my father's .38 from under the cellar stairs.

But I'd have to go through the living room to reach the cellar door.

No, I wouldn't. There was another way.

I could go around to the back of the house and sneak in through the outside cellar door.

Then I could get the gun and come up the stairs to the living room. I could throw open the door and catch Looney Tunes off guard. He was sitting with his back to the cellar door right now. How fast could he turn around anyway?

It could work.

Except . . .

What if, when I was in the cellar, Looney Tunes got up and moved to some other part of the room? What if he was looking right at the cellar door when I came up the stairs? He'd shoot me right between the eyes.

Unless I got him first.

I'd never shot a gun in my life. Was it hard to do? Did you just point it and pull the trigger? Probably. But maybe you had to cock it with your thumb and get it ready? Maybe there was some kind of safety catch you had to unlock. Where would that be? Would the gun jam? How about bullets? Was it loaded? I'd never looked.

What if the gun was loaded, and it wasn't locked, and there wasn't any safety catch, and I aimed it at Looney Tunes and pulled the trigger, and it didn't jam, it fired—and missed?

I'd be killed, and my father with me.

I was scared. Really scared.

I wiped the rain off my neck, but it just kept coming down.

There was one other thing I could do. Another choice.

I could get on my bike and ride away. Far away, to where it was safe. So far away it wouldn't be my fault, whatever happened at this house.

I could ride down to the Yellow Brick Road. It would probably be dry in there, where the trees and vines shut off the sky. I could just wait there, listening to the rain hitting the leaves overhead.

I probably wouldn't even hear the sound of a gun in the distance.

Or if I did hear it, maybe it wouldn't sound like a gun at all.

Just the wind snapping a dry branch off an old tree.

CHAPTER 16

The Cellar

Then I was running, crouched low, across the lawn to the side of the porch and around to the cellar door at the back of the house.

What made me do it, I guess, was thinking about the Yellow Brick Road, and then what it was I wanted the most.

Courage.

I was sick of being afraid. I didn't want to be that way anymore. I wanted to be tough and brave. Or at least have Rootie think that I was. And whatever was going to happen, I wanted to get it over with.

Nobody saw me, I guess, because when I got the cellar door open, I could hear Looney Tunes talking as if nothing special was going on.

I went down the cellar steps. It was dark because of the rainy day. I couldn't see anything. The floor was concrete. If I knocked something over, it would make a big noise. So I moved along very slowly, taking little steps with my hands out, feeling my way.

Something metal. I ran my fingers over it. Metal, with a rounded edge. Some kind of tub . . . A wheelbarrow.

I went around the wheelbarrow's wooden handles and almost stumbled over a tangle of garden hose.

Looney Tunes's voice was coming through the floorboards just over my head now. It was a wet, phlegmy voice, and I could imagine bubbles of spit gathering at the sides of his mouth. Every so often he coughed a deep, raspy cough.

"We're getting old, Harry," said Looney Tunes. "You know? You feel it on the stairs. The legs go. At this age you have to start to take care of yourself a little more. Go to the gym. Lift weights. Join a health club. Eat right. Low fat. I used to work out. But then I had a little heart problem a couple of years ago. So it was better not to overdo. I take medication. I try to walk every day. Here and there. Another thing, your memory goes. You don't recall. Maybe that's good."

Then I heard my father's voice. It was shaky.

"Frankie," said my father, "we go back a long way, you and me. A long way."

"Harry," said Looney Tunes, "I got a job to do. You can understand that."

Nobody said anything. Somebody shifted their feet. The cellar was full of cigar smell.

My father spoke again. "I understand your position, Frankie. I understand completely. But why don't we talk? Why don't old friends talk? There could be other ways. We could discuss other ways."

"There's no other way," said Looney Tunes. "If I don't do what I'm given to do, then I'm going to be in trouble. Like you, Harry. Disloyal. Betraying the trust they placed in me. And they're going to have to send somebody after *me*. You can see the logic."

"Yes, but—"

"My ass is on the line, Harry."

"Frankie," said my father, "I have a son. A boy. Eleven years old."

"Shut up, Harry," said Looney Tunes. "You're going to piss me off."

I moved ahead. I edged around a stack of paint cans and went down a narrow alley between a couple of chairs and some shutters leaning against the wall.

When Looney Tunes spoke again, his voice was softer. Like talking to a friend again. "This is my last job anyway," he said. "Absolutely. I don't need this aggravation. I'm going to retire. I deserve a rest. I did what they wanted all these years, now it's their turn to provide." There was a scratching sound. Maybe Looney Tunes was using a wooden match. He began to cough. The cough went on and on. Finally Looney Tunes caught his breath. "I'm thinking Gulf Coast—Alabama. I've seen brochures. I hear good things. You can pick up an attractive home without paying an arm and a leg, like in Florida."

I stepped on something. It was the end of a rake. I had stepped on the prongs, and the handle came flying out from the wall. I caught it just in time.

I hoped the gun would still be where I'd hidden it. But maybe my father had found it and taken it back. I could see a thin edge of light around the cellar door. I was only a few yards from the stairs. I moved very slowly and carefully.

My toe touched the bottom step. The gun would be just behind it—if it was there—under the bag of grass seed.

I leaned over and reached out.

Before I could pull back, my fingers had tapped something hard and knocked it over. I knew right away exactly what it was.

Glass.

My father must have put his empty bottles on the stairs. They went down like duckpins. The racket was insane. Bottles clinking, toppling, clattering, crashing down the steps and exploding on the concrete floor.

I jumped back, and then the cellar door burst open and there was light everywhere. Looney was at the top of the stairs, the gun in his hand. I turned and ran. He began firing, and as I passed the wheelbarrow it must have been hit, because it threw itself against the wall: *Clang!* Then a stack of flowerpots on a shelf jumped and shattered.

I ran up the steps and out the door onto the lawn and across the grass to the woods. Then I was tearing through briars and slipping on wet rocks and swerving around tree trunks until I saw the beech tree ahead. I ran around the far side and climbed as fast as I could up the steps to The Ship. It seemed to take forever. My feet kept slipping, but at last I got to the top and threw myself onto the deck.

My heart was hammering, and I was breathing so loudly I was afraid it could be heard all the way back at the house. I tried to take little gasps of air, spacing them apart and then letting them out slowly, but it didn't work.

Then I heard my father yell. "Look out, Pete!" he shouted. "He's coming!" It sounded as if he was on the porch, and then there was a gunshot. My father gave a howl, and there was a thud.

Then I heard footsteps down below. Branches cracking. The footsteps came toward the tree. Maybe Looney Tunes wouldn't see the wooden steps nailed to the tree. Maybe he would just go by.

Suddenly there was silence. He had seen the steps and where they led.

A scraping sound. Then another.

He was climbing up.

I put my hands over my ears and shut my eyes as tight as I could.

The Ladder

A hand grabbed my shoulder. I jumped.

It was Rootie.

"Take it easy," she whispered. "Are you okay?"

"Yes," I whispered. "Where'd you come from?"

Rootie climbed onto the deck and flopped down next to me. "I followed you after you'd left. I was right at the edge of the woods when the shooting started. I saw you come out of the cellar. I knew where you were headed."

"Do you think he'll find us?" I whispered.

"Maybe," she whispered. She was shaking.

We heard heavy steps moving into the woods. They seemed to be going away from us. Then they stopped. Looney Tunes coughed for a while. Then the steps started again.

This time they were coming toward us.

Rootie clutched my hand and squeezed it so hard I almost yelled. We looked at each other. Her eyes were very wide. Now I was shaking all over, just like Rootie, and I couldn't stop.

The steps came closer—crunching on the leaves, breaking twigs. Closer and closer.

Silence again.

We could hear him breathing. Right under the tree house.

He began to climb the steps. The breathing got louder.

A huge hand came over the edge of the deck, groping. Only a couple of feet from our faces.

It came crawling toward us like a fat hairless tarantula, creeping across the boards.

Then Looney's enormous pasty face slid up above the side, coming up like a moon. His hat was gone, and his orange toupee had turned sideways on his head.

"Get down out of here," he said. His other hand swung up, holding the black gun. "Fast," he said, and then the gun was pointed right at me.

"We're coming," I said. Rootie and I got up on our hands and knees and turned around. Suddenly there was a sound of wood splitting. Even before I looked back, I knew what it was: One of the steps on the tree trunk had given way, and now Looney Tunes was falling backward through the air. An instant later we heard a crack and a thud.

Rootie and I didn't move. We just listened for the next sound.

There wasn't any sound after that. Only the rain spattering the deck of The Ship.

"Look over the edge and see what happened," whispered Rootie.

"*You* look," I said.

"I'm scared to look," she whispered.

"So am I," I said. "He's probably just waiting for us."

"Let's *both* look," said Rootie. "At the same time."

"Okay," I said. We moved slowly along on our elbows until we reached the edge. "Ready?" I whispered.

"One . . . two . . . three . . . Look!" whispered Rootie.

We both stuck our heads out and looked down.

"Oh my god," said Rootie.

Looney Tunes was lying face up on a big rock, his legs bent like somebody resting on a beach. One hand was on his chest, as if he was reaching for something in his coat. The other arm was stretched out above his head, palm up, almost as if he was waving good-bye. His head was at a weird angle, looking downward to one side—like somebody trying to remember something from a long time ago.

Rootie and I climbed down from The Ship.

My father came limping through the woods. His leg was bloody. "Are you all right?" he said. "I tried to warn you. Did you hear me yell? I grabbed him and tried to stop him, then he shot me."

I didn't say anything.

We stood looking at the body.

"He's gone," said Rootie.

"Bastard," said my father.

"His head must have hit the rock," I said.

Rootie looked at me. "Weren't you scared to go into the cellar?" she asked.

"Yes," I said. "But I was more scared what would happen if I didn't."

"I think it was brave," said Rootie. "Definitely."

"Thanks," I said.

I took a last look at Looney Tunes. Rain was coming down on his bald head. His toupee was off to one side, lying upside down on the ground like a road kill.

C H A P T E R   1 8

Leaving

Last night was the first time in the month since Looney Tunes died that I got through the night without a nightmare. I always had a scary dream, and woke up, and had to get up and walk around for a while, trying to get away from it so I could sleep. But the dreams were like the briars in the woods behind our house—they snagged you and tore at you and wouldn't let you go. Sometimes the dreams were shipwrecks in the snow, and sometimes they were people shooting guns. Sometimes it was a dream I'd had before, and that was the worst one: I was walking along a beach below a cliff, and when I looked up, the white bones began to come slowly out of the clay, and I knew they were coming to get me, but my feet were stuck in the sand.

But at last I had slept through the night, and maybe it was because I knew we were leaving the island today: Mrs. Bowditch, Rootie, and I.

We're going to stay at Mrs. Bowditch's house in New York for a while. Rootie's going to show me around what she and her grandmother call "the city." What they mean is Manhattan. I guess they never go to any other part. Rootie knows the buses and the Lexington Avenue subway, and how to whistle through her fingers for a taxi.

When September comes, I don't know what will happen. Maybe I could go to school where Rootie goes, until my father got settled, at least.

After Looney Tunes got killed, there was a story about him in the papers. They said he was "a reputed hit man for the mob," and he had a long record and a bunch of names like Frank Smith and Frank Stone, and nicknames like Cueball, and the Angel. They said he died in a fall—an accident.

A couple of FBI men came and talked to me for a long time. They told me they're going to move my father to some place where they can protect him. The deal is, he's promised to be a witness and testify in court about the people he knows and what they've done. It's the witness protection program. I'd heard of that before.

Mrs. Bowditch and Rootie came by around nine this morning to pick me up. Mrs. Bowditch was driving her old Buick convertible—it was cream colored, maybe forty years old, and the top was down. We were going to catch the ten o'clock boat.

I said good-bye to my father on the front porch. He walks with a cane now. He was trembly, and he hadn't shaved, but he gave me a hug. That was pretty unusual. Maybe even the first time. And when he did, I felt how really thin he was, and how his ribs stuck out, and all of a sudden I didn't want to leave him.

"Take care of yourself, Pete," he said. He looked away. "Go on—they're waiting for you."

I ran down the steps and climbed into the back of the Buick, and I didn't look at our house until the car was pretty far down the road. Then I turned and looked, but there wasn't anything to see. If my father had stayed on the porch at all, maybe wondering if I was going to wave to him—

and maybe he was ready to wave to me—he must have given up and gone inside. Nobody was there.

Mrs. Bowditch drove the Buick aboard the ferryboat, and then we climbed up to the passenger deck and stood at the stern railing as the boat got ready to leave the slip. Mrs. Bowditch had brought what she called a hamper—a little wicker suitcase. She sat down on a bench and began to unpack it. First she took out a small red tablecloth. Then plates and cups and red napkins. On each plate she put a sandwich wrapped in waxed paper. Then she took out a thermos bottle and filled the cups. "Lunch whenever!" she called to us.

The ferryboat began to rumble. The ship's horn gave a blast, and we all jumped. A deckhand closed the gate, and the ferryboat moved quickly away from the shore. The water was smooth. Big clouds were heaped up like Reddi-

Wip. A bunch of screeching seagulls floated above us, leaning on the breeze, hoping for scraps, and the wake from the boat went tumbling away until it flattened out in long streamers pointing back at the island.

Rootie and I stood together, watching. I looked at the Bayview Hotel on the hill, and I remembered how I used to ride my bike up there and watch for the ferry. Now it was just the opposite: I was on the ferry, looking at the hotel.

It got smaller and smaller, and then the island began to shrink, too. We sat on the bench and ate the sandwiches—BLTs, and really good—with Mrs. Bowditch.

The boat must have been moving fast, or maybe we spent a long time having our picnic, but by the time Rootie and I looked again, we couldn't see the island anymore.